Naughty Chérie!

By Joyce Carol Oates
Illustrated by Mark Graham

HarperCollinsPublishers

For Evan, and for Little Chérie
—J.C.O.

For Josh
—M.G.

NAUGHTY CHÉRIE!

Library of Congress Cataloging-in-Publication Data ▪ Oates, Joyce Carol, date. ▪ Naughty Chérie! / by Joyce Carol Oates ; illustrated by Mark Graham.— 1st ed. ▪   p.   cm. ▪   Summary: Chérie loves being the naughtiest kitten until she meets a group of rowdy animals who show her that being naughty is not always that nice. ▪ ISBN-10: 0-06-074358-1 (trade bdg.) — ISBN-13: 978-0-06-074358-1 (trade bdg.) ▪ ISBN-10: 0-06-074359-X (lib. bdg.) — ISBN-13: 978-0-06-074359-8 (lib. bdg.) ▪ [1. Behavior—Fiction. 2. Cats—Fiction. 3. Animals—Infancy—Fiction.] I. Graham, Mark, date, ill. II. Title. ▪ PZ7.O1056Nau 2008   2005017790 ▪ [E]—dc22   CIP ▪ AC ▪ Designed by Stephanie Bart-Horvath ▪ 1 2 3 4 5 6 7 8 9 10 ▪ ❖ ▪ First Edition

Little Chérie was the prettiest of Momma Cat's five kittens. She had the longest eyelashes and the softest hair and the fluffiest tail and the prettiest markings. Little Chérie was always being kissed and petted and given extra treats because she was so pretty.

Momma Cat and her five little kittens lived with the Smiths in their house on Lakeside Avenue. Mr. and Mrs. Smith had one little girl—Evan.

Evan loved Momma Cat and all the kittens, but Little Chérie was Evan's favorite. You could roll a ball anywhere and Little Chérie would always find it. And little Chérie would roll the ball back to you!

When Evan practiced piano, Little Chérie would practice too!
There were two strange things about Little Chérie, though.
Little Chérie never purred like the other kittens—
                    —and Little Chérie was very naughty.

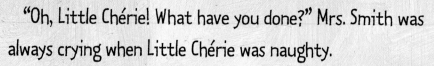

"Oh, Little Chérie! What have you done?" Mrs. Smith was always crying when Little Chérie was naughty.

Little Chérie sneaked in front of her brothers and sisters and gobbled up all their snacks!

Little Chérie climbed into the piano and played the strings from the inside!

Little Chérie climbed up
Mrs. Smith's new curtains and
brought them crashing down!

When Evan read her favorite story to Little Chérie,
Little Chérie's tail began to twitch, and suddenly Little
Chérie jumped on the book and tore the pages.

Evan said, "Oh, Chérie! What a naughty
kitten you are!" Evan felt very bad,
because she loved the book that
Grandma had given her.

Little Chérie was always sorry
for being naughty. Evan forgave
her with a kiss.

One rainy morning Little Chérie could not go outside to play. You could see that Little Chérie was restless, because her tail twitched.

Little Chérie spilled
the kittens' water dish!

Little Chérie attacked
Mr. Smith's shoelaces!

Although she knew that the dining-
room table was forbidden to all kittens,
Little Chérie went exploring!

When Little Chérie ran to hide, she woke
Evan from her nap.
"Oh, Little Chérie! What have you done?"
Mrs. Smith cried.

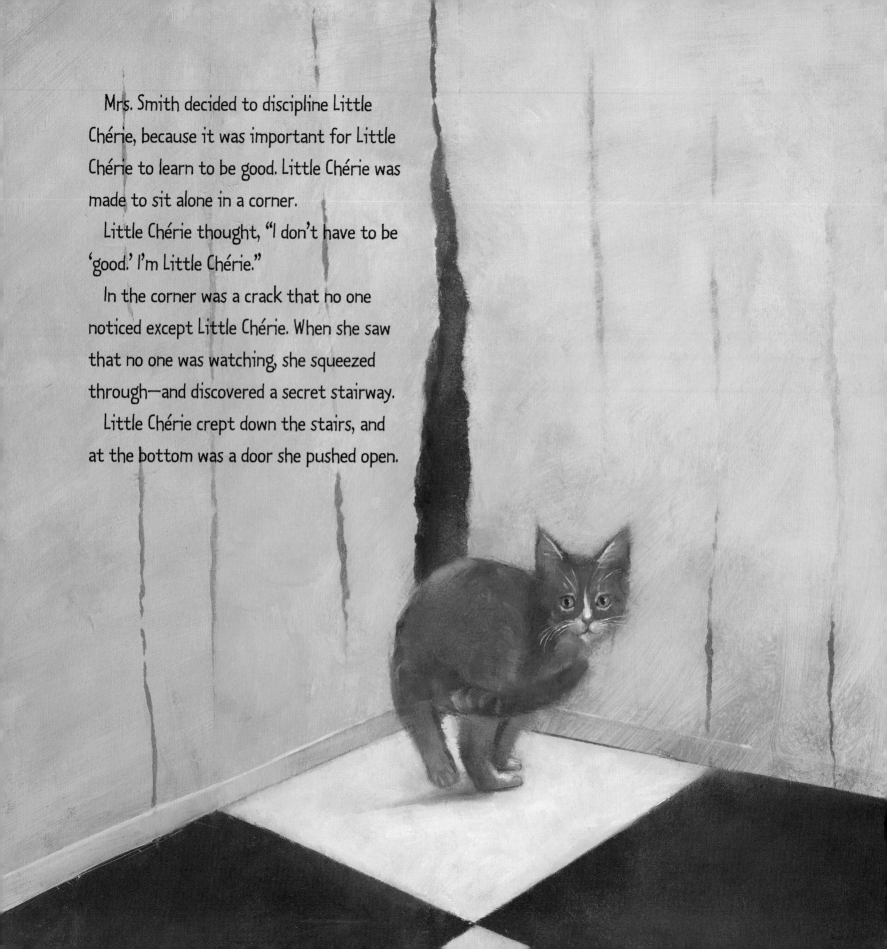

Mrs. Smith decided to discipline Little Chérie, because it was important for Little Chérie to learn to be good. Little Chérie was made to sit alone in a corner.

Little Chérie thought, "I don't have to be 'good.' I'm Little Chérie."

In the corner was a crack that no one noticed except Little Chérie. When she saw that no one was watching, she squeezed through—and discovered a secret stairway.

Little Chérie crept down the stairs, and at the bottom was a door she pushed open.

What a strange, happy place! Little Chérie had never been in this place before.

LITTLE FRIENDS KINDERCARE

There was a baby elephant! There was a baby ostrich! There was a baby giraffe, and a baby monkey, and a baby panda! There were too many babies for Little Chérie to count.

The animal babies were very friendly. When they saw their new visitor, they hurried to say hello.

"My name is Elfia," said the baby elephant.
"My name is Ozzie," said the baby ostrich.
"My name is Gerard," said the baby giraffe.
"My name is Mikey," said the baby monkey.
"My name is Algernon," said the baby panda.

Little Chérie was feeling shy, for she was so much smaller than her new friends. She hoped Elfia wouldn't step on her!

"My name is Little Chérie," Little Chérie said. "I live upstairs."

All the animals wanted to pet Little Chérie, because she was so pretty. Algernon said, "I never saw a kitten before."

Elfia said, "Chérie, would you like to ride on my back?"

Before Little Chérie could answer, Elfia lifted her in her trunk and placed Little Chérie on her back.

"Elfia, that's naughty," said
Gerard, the baby giraffe. But Gerard
was laughing more than scolding.
  Mikey said, "Would you like to
dance with me, Chérie?"
  Before Little Chérie could answer,
Mikey swung down to grab her.

"Mikey, that was naughty!" said Ozzie, the
baby ostrich. But Ozzie was laughing.
  Little Chérie was very thirsty. But Algernon
spilled the water bowl.

It was playtime. But Gerard climbed up the slide ahead of Little Chérie and tipped it over!

Mikey said, "Come play with me, Chérie! I'm not clumsy." But Mikey
was very skilled at climbing and swinging on the monkey bars, while
Little Chérie lost her balance and almost fell.

All the animals cried, "Mikey, that's very naughty! You must learn
to be good."

"I don't have to be 'good,'" Mikey boasted. "I'm a monkey."

When it was nap time, Ozzie pecked at
Little Chérie and would not let her sleep.

When it was snack time, each of the baby animals had ice cream. But Elfia gobbled up her own ice cream and then Little Chérie's. "Oh, Elfia!" the baby animals scolded. "That's naughty."

Elfia blinked her long eyelashes to show she was sorry, but Little Chérie could see that Elfia wasn't sorry at all.

By this time Little Chérie was feeling
very hungry, very tired, and very sad! She
missed Momma Cat and her sisters and
brothers, and most of all she missed Evan.
She crept off into a corner, and there was
the stairway back home, and the crack!

This was strange: No one seemed to have noticed that Little Chérie had been away. Mrs. Smith was saying, "Little Chérie, what a good kitten you've been! You can leave the corner now."

It was dinnertime. Little Chérie was going to push ahead of the other kittens, because she was very hungry, but she remembered how naughty the baby animals had been, and so she did not but waited her turn.

The next day, when Mrs. Smith put up her new curtains, Little Chérie was tempted to climb up on them—but she did not.

When Evan practiced piano, Little Chérie was
tempted to jump inside the piano—but she did not.

Mrs. Smith said, "Little Chérie, you have been such a good kitten, Evan has a surprise for you."

It was Little Chérie's favorite treat: ice cream.
Suddenly, Little Chérie purred. She purred to thank Mrs. Smith,
and she purred to thank Evan.

That night, Little Chérie slept beside Evan on her pillow. She purred through the night, and her tail did not twitch even once!